The Littles Have a Wedding

BY JOHN PETERSON
PICTURES BY ROBERTA CARTER CLARK

SCHOLASTIC INC.
New York Toronto London Auckland Sydney

ISBN 0-590-40135-1

Text copyright © 1971 by John Peterson.
Illustrations copyright © 1971 by Scholastic Books, Inc.
All rights reserved. Published by Scholastic Inc.

12 11 10 9 8 7 6 5 4 3   0 1/9

Printed in the U.S.A.   28

To my mother

"TOM! LUCY!" Mr. Little called down to his children through the hole in the roof.

"Yes, Dad," Tom Little called back from inside the attic of the house.

"Uncle Pete and I have hold of the strap," Mr. Little said. "When I say 'go,' you push and we'll pull on the strap."

"Lucy and I are all set, Dad," said Tom.

"Ready . . . set . . . GO!" Mr. Little said.

Mr. Little and Uncle Pete pulled hard on the strap. A pair of black binoculars came through the hole in the roof. Tom Little, aged ten, and his younger sister, Lucy, scrambled through the hole after the binoculars.

Mr. Little slid a shingle back into place to cover the hole in the roof. "Now," he said, "let's get these binoculars up to the chimney for a look around."

Mr. Little and Uncle Pete got hold of the heavy end of the binoculars. Tom and Lucy took the light end. It was hard work for the four of them to drag the binoculars up to the top of the roof.

The Littles were tiny people. They weren't just small. They were tiny, about as long as a pencil. Mr. Little was the tallest Little and he was only six inches tall. His daughter, Lucy, was less than four inches tall. Her little sister, Baby Betsy, who was about six months old, was no bigger than a thimble.

The Littles looked like ordinary people except for one thing: they had tails. They weren't useful tails. But they did look pretty, the Littles thought. And they took good care of their tails. Lucy sometimes wore a ribbon on hers.

The Little family made their home in the walls of George Bigg's house. They lived in ten small rooms that took up very little space. They always kept out of sight when the Biggs were around. The Biggs never found out the Littles lived in the same house with them.

"Now, Tom," Mr. Little said, "Uncle Pete and I will hold the binoculars off the roof. You climb up the chimney and hang the strap over the television antenna."

Tom scrambled up the chimney with the strap. Soon the binoculars were swinging free under the antenna. They could be turned easily in any direction.

"I hope these binoculars aren't too heavy for the TV antenna," said Mr. Little.

"We wouldn't want to lose Mr. Bigg's binoculars."

Tom and Lucy looked into one lens. "Hey, Dad!" Tom said, "We've got to focus this thing. It's all blurry."

"It makes me dizzy," Lucy said.

"First, let's turn the binoculars to face east," said Mr. Little. "Cousin Dinky went that way when he left three weeks ago."

"I still say he's not lost," said Uncle Pete, "and nothing has happened to him.

He's out there somewhere in the Big Valley having an adventure. Dinky can take care of himself, just as I could when I was adventuring."

Mr. Little looked through the binoculars at the houses and trees that were farthest away. "We're lucky George Bigg's house is the highest one around," he said. "We get a good view from here." Mr. Little turned the ring that focused the binoculars.

"It's clear now," said Tom. "Gee! We can see so far."

"You may be right about Dinky being okay, Uncle Pete. I hope you are," said Mr. Little. "But it's not like him to stay away so long." Mr. Little turned the binoculars slowly. "If his glider has crashed in a tree or on a rooftop, we might be able to see it through these binoculars."

"Oh, Daddy!" Lucy said. "I wish you wouldn't talk about Cousin Dinky that way."

"I'm sorry, Lucy," said Mr. Little, "but we must face facts."

The four tiny people looked through the binoculars all that afternoon. They looked in every direction for a sign of the missing glider pilot.

It was almost suppertime. Lucy left to help her mother get their supper from the Biggs' leftover food. Uncle Pete and Mr. Little sat down to rest against the chimney. Tom was left alone looking through the binoculars. Suddenly he yelled, "Hey! I see something!"

The two men ran to the binoculars. "Look next to that tall tree near that red house," Tom said. "There's something shiny flying through the air. The sun just hit it."

"By golly!" said Uncle Pete. "I believe that's Dinky's glider."

"It is! It is!" Mr. Little said. "He's flying this way. Thank heavens!"

"Doesn't he have someone with him in the glider?" said Tom.

"He does," Uncle Pete said. "And whoever he is, he sure has long hair."

"It's a lady," Tom said.

"A lady?" said Uncle Pete. He looked long and carefully through the binoculars. "It *is* a woman, by jinks! Now why in the world would Dinky be out on an adventure with a woman?"

Just then the sound of fire engines came from somewhere in the Big Valley.

Mr. Little looked up from the binoculars. He saw black smoke rising from a house a few blocks away. "This is terrible!" he said. "That's the house where the Fines live."

"Look at all that smoke," said Uncle Pete. "That's a bad fire."

Tom was still looking through the binoculars. "Cousin Dinky sees the fire too," he said. "Now he's flying toward it."

Mr. Little turned the binoculars toward

the fire. It was hard to see anything through the smoke. But when the wind blew some of it away for a moment, he saw some tiny people standing on the roof. "It's the Fines!" he said. "It looks as if the whole family is trapped on the roof."

Flames were coming out of the upstairs windows.

"Where's Dinky now?" said Uncle Pete. "I can't see him."

"There he is," Mr. Little said, looking through the binoculars. "He's going for a landing. He's going to try to save them."

The Littles watched Cousin Dinky's glider disappear into the thick black smoke.

They waited.

Finally Tom said, "Can you see him, Dad? I can't."

"No — too much smoke," said Mr. Little. "He's probably landed on the roof by now."

"By golly," Uncle Pete said. "That Dinky sure is the brave one."

"Is it possible for him to take out all four Fines in one trip?" Mr. Little said. "I doubt if there's time for two trips."

"Here he comes!" Tom shouted.

The glider came sailing out of the smoke. The Littles saw that the Fines were aboard. One of them was hanging onto the wing.

"Hurrah!" yelled Uncle Pete. "They're safe!"

"Oh gosh!" said Tom. "The glider is on fire."

Smoke and flames trailed out behind the glider. It nosed toward the ground. The Littles watched in silence as Cousin Dinky's glider disappeared behind the trees near the burning house.

VERY EARLY the next morning the Little family gathered in their living room. Uncle Pete sat on the sofa. Baby Betsy crawled into his lap. "We've waited long enough for Dinky to get here," he said. "It's time to go looking for him."

"As soon as we saw the crash we should have gone to help," said Tom.

"We're not *sure* there was a crash. We didn't *see* one," Mr. Little said. "Besides it would have been too dark for us to look for anyone — and too dangerous. I thought it would be best to wait and see if Dinky got back on his own."

Mr. Little looked at the pocket watch that hung over the fireplace. "I think we should stick to our plan. If Cousin Dinky doesn't get here in the next half hour, we should start after him."

"He must have crashed," Uncle Pete said. He shook his head as though it were hard to believe.

"How could Cousin Dinky crash?" Lucy said. "I don't believe it. He's such a good pilot." She looked around the room at the gloomy faces. "How could he crash?"

Granny Little sat in her rocking chair. She was knitting a sweater for Baby Betsy. "I don't think we should give up hope," she said. "Dinky has been on many dangerous adventures."

"We saw the glider with its tail on fire," Tom said.

Granny Little nodded her head. "Dinky might have landed safely anyway," she said.

"I wonder who the young woman was," said Mrs. Little. She sat next to Uncle Pete on the sofa and looked up at the watch.

"What young woman?" Uncle Pete said.

"She's probably a girl friend of Dinky's," Granny Little said.

"Oh, *that* young woman!" said Uncle Pete. He stood up and limped back and forth in front of the fireplace. (He had been wounded in the Mouse Invasion of '35 and had to use a cane.)

"That's silly talk! Dinky doesn't have a girl friend. He doesn't have time — too busy adventuring!" Uncle Pete sat down. "Why, just being the mailman for all the tiny people in the Big Valley takes up most of his time," he went on. "Then — the rest of the time he's off exploring new places and finding people in danger and saving them."

Granny Little laughed. "Oh, Peter Little!" she said. "Most young men find time for girl friends. And Dinky is so romantic!" She sighed. "Just to hear him sing and play his guitar would make most any girl like him."

The rest of the Littles tried to keep from laughing. Everyone except Granny Little knew that Cousin Dinky couldn't even carry a tune very well. But Granny Little was hard of hearing. She liked Cousin Dinky and enjoyed hearing him sing. Her family didn't have the heart to tell her he had a terrible singing voice.

Granny Little smiled to herself as she thought of Cousin Dinky singing and playing his guitar. She nodded her head. "He'll find a nice girl and they'll want to get married," she said. "Probably sooner than we think."

"Ho! Ho!" Uncle Pete said. "It will never happen. Dinky's a real bachelor, if I ever saw one. And I ought to know one when I see one — being one myself."

"Dinky doesn't care about getting married," Tom said. "He told me so."

"He does so care about getting married," Lucy said. "He said he wished *I* was old enough. He'd marry me!"

Everybody laughed.

"HALLO!" The voice came from outside the apartment in the wall passageway. "Anybody home?"

"It's Cousin Dinky!" Tom yelled. He ran to the door and opened it.

"Thank heavens!" Mrs. Little said.

"Good!" said Granny Little.

Lucy ran to the door. "I knew it!"

Cousin Dinky and a young woman stood in the doorway. Their faces were streaked with soot and their clothes were torn.

Lucy threw herself at Cousin Dinky. He lifted her high in the air and then hugged her.

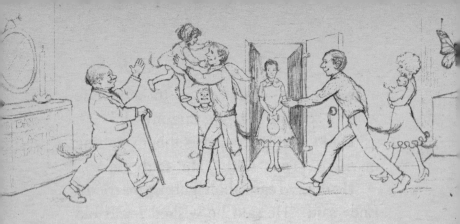

"I knew you were all right," Lucy said.

"Dinky! Thank goodness you're alive," said Mr. Little.

Cousin Dinky looked surprised. "Why, of course I'm alive, Uncle Will," he said. "Why shouldn't I be?" He was holding the young woman's hand. He led her into the room. "I'd like all of you to meet Della Kett. You remember the Ketts. They live at the far end of the valley."

"Who is she?" said Granny Little. She cupped her ear to hear better.

"It's the Ketts' little girl, Della," Mr. Little said. "Only she's not a little girl any more."

The Littles introduced themselves to Della Kett.

"Dinky has told me all about you," she said.

"We're so happy to see you weren't hurt," said Mr. Little. Then he explained how they had watched the rescue of the Fines through Mr. Bigg's binoculars.

"The Fines are okay," said Cousin Dinky. "We went back to the house. The fire wasn't as bad as it looked. Their apartment is in perfect shape except for the smoke smell."

"The glider burned up on the ground," said Della. She shrugged her shoulders. "No water."

"Lucky I've got another glider half made," Cousin Dinky said.

Cousin Dinky went into the hall passageway and came back with his guitar. "And now for the great news," he said. "Lucky for me this guitar didn't burn in the glider."

"Oh, you saved that guitar, did you?" Uncle Pete said.

"I need this guitar to tell you the great news," Cousin Dinky said. "I have written a new song about my latest adventure at the Ketts, and I would like to sing it for you."

"Ah . . . couldn't you just tell us?" said Uncle Pete.

"This is an important adventure, Uncle Pete," Cousin Dinky said. "I just had to write a song about it. Such a wonderful adventure! It's the only way to tell you."

"Sit down everyone," Granny Little said. "Let's have a little quiet — I want to hear every word."

The Littles sat in chairs around the room. Della Kett sat on the floor near Cousin Dinky who took a footstool. He picked up his guitar and sang:

Yes, yes, yes,
You'll never guess
I found a maiden in distress,
Stuck on a thistle bush where she might die.
I lowered my flaps — flew down from the sky.

Yes, yes, yes,
You'll never guess
I saved a maiden in distress.
I flew her home to her Mom and Dad.
They'd missed her so and were very glad.

Yes, yes, yes,
You'll never guess
I loved that maiden in distress.
I stayed two weeks near Della's side
And finally asked her to be my bride.

Yes, yes, yes,
You'll never guess
I'll marry that maiden in distress.
I asked her always to share my life —
To fly with me and be my wife.

Yes, yes, yes
Now, did you guess?
The maiden answered, "Yes! Yes! Yes!"

"Oh my!" Mrs. Little said. "We're going to have a wedding. How nice."

Mr. Little jumped up and shook Cousin Dinky's hand. "Good luck to both of you," he said.

"I knew it when you walked in the door," said Granny Little to Della Kett. "Bless you, my dear."

"But what about your adventures?" said Uncle Pete to Cousin Dinky. "If you go through with this wedding, you'll have to give up having adventures."

"Not me," Cousin Dinky said. "I'll always have adventures."

"You'll have to settle down," said Uncle Pete. He looked at Della. "Won't he?"

"Not me," said Cousin Dinky. "Adventuring is in my blood. I'll be off on an adventure right after the wedding."

Della laughed. "We had our first fight over Dinky's adventures," she said. "I told him I wouldn't marry him if he didn't settle down. But after what happened yesterday, that's all changed."

"I'm going to write a new song about that," Cousin Dinky said.

"We were flying along and arguing about whether Dinky should have adventures after the wedding," Della said. "Then we saw the fire. Dinky thought the Fines might be caught in the fire."

"Della told me to fly over to the fire and find out," Cousin Dinky said. "I told her it would be dangerous and that I wouldn't take her to a dangerous place if I didn't have to."

"I said to him that if he didn't get over there and rescue the Fines, I'd be mad at him," said Della.

"And that's how we had our first adventure together," said Cousin Dinky.

"I loved it!" Della said. "Why, we flew

right into that fire and smoke, and rescued the Fine family. I never enjoyed anything so much in my life."

"Della wants us to go on an adventure for our honeymoon," Cousin Dinky said.

The Littles laughed.

"I tried to tell her I can't *order* an adventure," said Cousin Dinky. "They just happen!"

"We'll have one for our honeymoon," said Della. "I know it."

ONE MONTH later Tom and Lucy were in Mrs. Bigg's jewelry box. They were trying to find an old gold watch she kept there. Tom said they could use it to help them make a wedding ring for Cousin Dinky to give Della.

"Ouch!" Tom said. "Hey! Some of this jewelry has sharp pins."

"I can't see very well inside this box, Tom," said Lucy. "Can't we open the lid a little more?"

"I'm trying to," said Tom. "Give me some help. The lid is heavy. Let's stick this earring in between the lid and the box to keep it open."

The Biggs were out of the house that day. Mrs. Bigg and her son, Henry, had gone to the amusement park for the afternoon.

"Ouch!" Lucy yelled. "You dropped the lid on my tail."

"You did that, Lucy," said Tom. "You're not holding up your end of the lid."

Tom gave the lid a big shove. He poked the earring into place. "There — now, let's find the watch."

Lucy patted her tail and made a face. "My tail still hurts," she said.

"Let's find that watch," said Tom. "We have to get out of here before Mrs. Bigg and Henry get back from the amusement park."

"Why can't we just take the watch and leave?" said Lucy.

"That's stealing," Tom said. "We only take leftovers, you know that." He dug into the pile of jewelry at the bottom of the box. "Here it is," he said. "Here's the old watch."

"Look at it," Lucy said. "The dial is broken — there aren't any hands. Isn't the watch a 'leftover'?"

"No," said Tom. "It's a 'keepsake.' I heard Mrs. Bigg tell Henry she likes to look at the watch now and then. It's solid gold! It used to belong to Mrs. Bigg's grandfather a long time ago. But we can take what we came after because it is inside the watch," Tom went on. "And Mrs. Bigg is never going to get that watch repaired. It's too heavy to carry, she says."

Tom climbed out onto Mrs. Bigg's dresser and found a small nail file. He used it as a lever to get the back off the watch.

"Oh!" said Lucy. "Look at those beautiful red jewels, Tom!"

"They're rubies," Tom said, "and there are twenty-one of them in the watch — see?"

"Won't Cousin Dinky be surprised," said Lucy, "when we show him a ring with one of these rubies on it?"

"Well, I'm the ring bearer," Tom said, "and it's my job to find a ring. I want Cousin Dinky to give Della a real special ring. She's keen!"

"She'll love it!" Lucy said.

Tom took a hat pin and dug at one of the jewels in the watch. He was trying to get it out of its place. "They're not screwed in place," Tom said. "They're just wedged in."

Tom grunted as he pushed. "I can't move it. Wow! Get on the end of the hat pin and help me, Lucy, will you?"

In a few minutes the ruby was out of the watch. Lucy picked up the jewel and turned it in her fingers. "Why are there jewels in watches anyway?" she said.

"They're harder than anything," Tom said. "They never wear out."

"Good!" Lucy said. "Our ring will last forever."

Tom pushed the lid of the jewelry box open so they could climb out. "Come on," he said. "Let's take it home and show everybody."

TOM AND LUCY ran into the Littles'
living room. The door slammed.

"Oh!" said Granny Little. She was
sewing in her rocking chair. "You made
me stick my finger."

Mrs. Little and Uncle Pete were sitting
on the sofa with Baby Betsy. The baby
was pulling on Uncle Pete's moustache.

"Isn't she smart?" Uncle Pete said.
"Most children her age couldn't do that,
could they?"

Tom held the ruby up for all to see.

"All we need to do now is find a ring to glue it to," he said.

"It's beautiful, Tom," Mrs. Little said. "I *do* hope you did the right thing — taking it."

"Mrs. Bigg won't miss it, Mother," said Tom. "Really."

"Won't it look wonderful on Della's finger?" Lucy said. She began to dance around the room. "We're going to have a wedding! We're going to have a wedding!"

Granny Little called to Mrs. Little. "Come over, will you, and hold Della's wedding dress up to you. You're about her size. I want to hem it."

Mrs. Little held the white dress to her shoulders. "What a wonderful idea," she said, "to make a wedding dress from this beautiful old ruffle."

"That's why I saved it when Mrs. Bigg threw her party dress out," Granny Little said. "I knew there'd be a wedding around here someday."

"Where did you and Dad get married, Mother?" Tom said.

"In a church down the block," said Mrs. Little. "It was quite a trip. That was before we could ride places on Hildy, the cat. We walked all the way. We were lucky though. The big people were having two weddings that month in the church. We had our pick."

"It was a beautiful wedding," Granny Little said. "And you and Will looked every bit as nice as the big bride and groom."

Uncle Pete pulled at his moustache. "It would be easier on everybody if Della got married in church. Why does she want a house wedding?"

"I've heard that house weddings are beautiful," said Mrs. Little.

"But, it's hard as all-get-out to find a house where the big people are going to have a wedding," Uncle Pete said. "It has to be a house where tiny people live too."

"Cousin Dinky will find a place," said Lucy. "He can do anything."

"Don't be too sure," said Uncle Pete. "He's been looking for almost a month with no luck. He's dog-boned tired."

"Oh, Dinky loves flying around in that new glider of his," Granny Little said. "Don't worry about him."

Tom said, "Why don't tiny people have their own ministers and justices of the peace to make marriages? Wouldn't it save a lot of trouble?"

"It *is* a lot of work, Tom," said Mrs. Little. "But most tiny people enjoy that kind of wedding. Usually they have to make a trip someplace in the Big Valley to get married. Friends are invited and they get to meet people they wouldn't see otherwise. Friendships are made that last a lifetime."

"That's how I met my oldest friend, Zelda Short," Granny Little said.

"Oh, I am so looking forward to a house

wedding," said Mrs. Little. "I hope it's close by so we can all go."

"Where is Della anyway?" Tom said.

"On the roof with your father," said Mrs. Little. "Cousin Dinky said he would try to fly by today and tell us if he has found a place for the wedding."

"Come on, Lucy!" Tom said. "Let's go up and watch."

"Tom, what about our ruby ring?" Lucy said. "Shouldn't we be looking for the ring part?"

"Oh, we have plenty of time for that," Tom said. "I don't want to miss the landing. I *love* to see Cousin Dinky land his glider on the roof."

"Please be careful up there, children," Mrs. Little said. "Especially if there's a wind."

TOM AND LUCY got into the tin-can elevator that went up to the roof. It was made from an old soup can and some pieces of string. Tom pulled on the string and slowly the elevator went up. The children found their father and Della on the roof. They were standing near the chimney.

"Any sign of Cousin Dinky?" asked Tom.

Mr. Little shook his head. He pointed to the setting sun. "It's going to be dark soon," he said.

"Dinky wouldn't fly in the dark," said Della. She looked worried.

A few minutes later Tom shouted: "There's Cousin Dinky! He's over the trees."

Everybody turned to look. Cousin Dinky's glider was riding the wind and coming toward them. It was clearing the trees at the edge of the yard.

Just then a car drove into the driveway below. It was Mrs. Bigg and Henry back from the amusement park.

"Oh, oh!" Della said. "What if they see Dinky land on the roof?"

Cousin Dinky's glider was coming straight toward the house. The Biggs' car was below and ahead of him.

The car stopped and Henry Bigg jumped out. His arms were full of toys and prizes.

Cousin Dinky's glider was almost over Henry's head.

Suddenly two toy balloons seemed to leap out of the car behind Henry. They shot up in the air. It looked as if they were going to hit the glider.

"Cousin Dinky doesn't see those balloons," Tom said.

"Watch out, Dinky!" Della wanted to close her eyes but she didn't.

Lucy grabbed her father's hand.

At the last moment Cousin Dinky saw the balloons coming up right in front of him. He grabbed at the controls. The tiny glider zoomed straight up and banked off to one side. The turn was too fast.

"Oh no!" said Della.

The glider hung in the air with its nose pointed up. Then it twisted and turned upside down. The glider went into a tailspin. It fell into the branches of a tall lilac bush near the house.

Henry Bigg walked on across the yard. The two gas-filled balloons bounced on the ends of long strings tied to Henry's wrists. He ran into the house, pulling the balloons after him.

Cousin Dinky climbed out of the glider and onto a branch of the lilac bush. A broken wing of the glider fluttered to the ground.

The Littles rushed to the edge of the roof and looked down.

Cousin Dinky was waving his arms in the air. "Good news!" he yelled. "I found a place. It's O.K. We're going to have a wedding!"

MRS. BIGG had picked up some Chinese food on the way home from the amusement park. So that night the Littles ate leftover egg-foo-young for supper.

Tom and Lucy found one leftover fortune cooky for the family. Lucy wished everyone would eat faster so they could see what the family fortune was.

"Isn't it wonderful?" said Cousin Dinky. "We're going to have our wedding at last, and at the home of our friends the Buttons."

"Hooray!" said Della. She clapped her hands.

"Only we'll have to hurry," said Cousin Dinky. "The wedding will take place tomorrow."

Mr. Little stopped eating. "Did you say tomorrow, Dinky?"

"It's crazy, I know," Cousin Dinky said. "But it happened fast. Remember the big girl at the Buttons — Vera Long? Well, she and Sam Tower have been going together for a long time. But they just suddenly decided to get married. And now they can't wait."

"I think that's cute," said Della.

"Haste makes waste," Uncle Pete said. "Remember that."

"It's settled then," said Cousin Dinky. "We go tonight."

"Tonight?" said Mrs. Little. "Oh dear, we're not ready."

"What am I going to wear, Mother?"

said Lucy. "I'm the flower girl. Do I have to wear my old white party dress?"

"What about presents for the bride and groom?" said Uncle Pete. "I thought we had plenty of time. I haven't got one yet."

"Oh, Peter!" Granny Little said. "Isn't that just like you to wait until the last minute."

"We'll have to go whether we're ready or not," Cousin Dinky said. "They're having the wedding tomorrow morning at ten o'clock."

"Ten o'clock!" Uncle Pete said. "We won't get any sleep."

"I won't sleep anyway," Della said. "I'm so nervous."

"I wanted to pick up Della's parents and my mother in the glider," Cousin Dinky said, "but now that it's broken, I won't be able to."

"We can visit them on our honeymoon," said Della, "after you fix the glider."

"I'll work on Lucy's dress on the way to the Buttons," Granny Little said, "if there's enough moonlight, and if I get to ride on Hildy, the cat. Maybe I can do something with that old dress to make it look different."

Mr. Little got up from the table. "We'd better start packing," he said. "Tom, find Hildy. Take her to the cellar. We'll leave from there."

Della jumped up and began taking dishes off the table. "I'll wash the dishes," she said.

"Wait, everyone!" said Lucy. "We forgot about the fortune cooky."

"I think Della should open it," Granny Little said.

"Yes, yes!" the Littles agreed.

Della Kett took a knife and began cutting pieces from the fortune cooky.

She passed them around the table. Then she reached into the cooky and pulled out a slip of paper with the fortune on it. She handed it to Lucy. "You read it, Lucy," she said. Then she smiled. "Maybe you'll bring us good luck."

Lucy read the fortune: "Haste makes waste!"

"Oh, my goodness!" said Mrs. Little. "Isn't that funny? That's just what Uncle Pete said."

"I did," Uncle Pete said. "And I meant it."

"It's only a fortune for fun," said Granny Little. "How could a piece of paper inside a cooky mean anything?"

"It's a sign," said Uncle Pete. "We're in too much of a hurry. I wonder if we shouldn't postpone the wedding. There will be another one along soon. Besides, I don't have a wedding present yet."

Everyone laughed.

"You don't have to be in a hurry to get us a present, Uncle Pete," said Della. "We're going to be married for a long time. We can wait."

An hour later Tom came back. "I can't find the cat," he said. "Maybe Mrs. Bigg let her out of the house."

"Then we'll have to walk," Mr. Little said. "There's no telling when she'll be back."

"What about the ring, Tom?" Lucy whispered. "When are we going to look for a ring for the ruby?"

"We'll have to wait until we get to the Buttons'," Tom said.

"Aw, Tom!" said Lucy.

"I'm the ring bearer, Lucy," said Tom. "I'll get the ring — don't worry."

IT WAS twelve o'clock midnight.

The Littles' suitcases were stacked in the center of the living room. They were taking enough clothes to stay for a few days.

Mrs. Little had awakened Baby Betsy who was crying. Della and Lucy were trying to quiet her down while Mrs. Little dressed her.

Mr. Little, Cousin Dinky, and Uncle Pete had their heads together in the corner of the room. They were talking in low voices. Tom was trying to hear what they were saying.

Suddenly Granny Little spoke up: "All right, you men, I know you're talking about me. Well, you can stop it! I'm going to the wedding and that's all there is to it. I can walk there just as well as anyone."

"Of course you're going," Mr. Little said. He walked over to the old lady. "It's just that we thought it would be more comfortable for you if you waited for Hildy to come back and made the trip on her. Tom and Uncle Pete can stay with you."

"What?" said Granny Little. "I might miss the wedding."

"Hildy could come back at any moment," said Mr. Little.

"If only I hadn't crashed the glider," Cousin Dinky said. "It would have been so easy to fly you over."

"What about using one of Henry's balloons?" said Tom.

"Balloons are too hard to control, Tom," said Cousin Dinky. "They just don't go the way you want them to."

"We'd end up in Timbuctoo," said Uncle Pete.

"I don't mean to *fly* in the balloon," Tom said. "If we tie a chair just under the balloon, Granny can sit in it. Then the rest of us can walk along and pull the string."

Cousin Dinky whistled. "Hey! That may be an idea, Tom!" He smiled at the others. "By golly, I think it might work."

"I can walk," said Granny Little. "What's all the fuss?"

"Maybe we can use both of the balloons," Cousin Dinky said. "We may not have to carry these suitcases."

"Someone help me," Tom said. He ran to the door. "I know where Henry tied them."

Granny Little began pulling snippets of material out of her sewing box. "I think I have just the thing to add to Lucy's white dress to give it a new and prettier look." Finally she held up a blue and white ribbon. "This French silk ribbon will make a beautiful blouse."

Lucy came running over. "Oh, Granny!" she said. "I love it!"

"You'll be the prettiest flower girl that ever was when I get through with this dress," said Granny Little. She sat right down and went to work.

Lucy danced around her grandmother's rocking chair. "I'll pick a violet on the way to the Buttons' house," she said. "It will go with the blue in the ribbon."

Uncle Pete stood near the fireplace. He was thinking hard. Suddenly he smiled. "I know just the thing for a wedding present!" he said. Then he limped over to where Della was helping Mrs. Little pack. "How would you and Dinky like a picture of President George Washington, my dear? I have a rare old ten cent stamp given to me by my grandfather. It's black — issued in 1847."

"Why, that sounds wonderful, Uncle Pete," Della said. "We could frame it and put it over the fireplace — when we get a fireplace."

A FEW HOURS later the Littles were
ready to start. They were just outside
the Biggs' house in the yard.

Tom and his father had tied baskets
to the two balloons. Granny Little sat
with Mrs. Little and Baby Betsy in one
of the baskets. The Littles' suitcases were
in the other basket under the second
balloon.

Some of Henry Bigg's marbles were
piled in the bottom of the baskets. Their
weight kept the balloons from flying
away.

Six strings hung down from the two baskets. The tiny people on the ground tied the strings around their waists. They were going to pull the balloons and baskets with them on the trip to the Buttons' house.

"Now," Mr. Little said, "take some of the marbles out of the baskets until the baskets go up in the air."

Soon the baskets were light enough for the balloons to lift them. They floated up until they were about ten inches off the ground.

"Great!" said Cousin Dinky. "It's going to work."

"Let's move out!" Mr. Little called. They all set off across the yard. The moon above the woods lighted their way.

"How's the ride up there?" Tom called to his mother and grandmother.

"Fine, Tom," said Granny Little from the balloon. "I'm sorry you all won't enjoy the trip as much as we will."

"We're up rather high, aren't we?" Mrs. Little said. "I'm not going to look down."

"Let's keep the talk down to a whisper," said Mr. Little. "We certainly don't want any animals or big people to see us."

"Umph!" said Uncle Pete. He patted a needle sword that was stuck in his belt. "Any animal that tries to monkey around with us will feel this inch of cold steel in his gizzard."

Almost everyone carried a weapon. Tom had a bow and arrows. Mr. Little carried a needle sword. Cousin Dinky and Della had spears. Lucy carried her favorite weapon: a pepper shaker. She had once saved the Littles from a weasel by shaking pepper into its eyes.

Even Mrs. Little carried a weapon: she had the broken tip of a kitchen knife in her belt. Granny Little refused to carry a weapon. "I never had to use one all the years I carried one," she said. "It's just extra weight."

The Littles crossed the Biggs' yard to the walnut tree. They were following Cousin Dinky's directions. He had made many hiking trips in the Big Valley, and so he knew the safest way.

They passed the walnut tree and entered a flower garden. It was early

June and the hollyhocks were beginning to bloom.

The giant flowers waved to and fro above them. A balloon brushed against a hollyhock, and a shower of pollen rained down on the Littles below.

"Aa-choo!" said Uncle Pete.

They left the flower garden to follow a path. After a long walk they came to the creek. There was a wooden foot bridge crossing it.

"Careful, everyone!" Cousin Dinky said. "Don't fall through the cracks in the bridge. There's a long two-foot drop to the water."

Tom looked down between the boards. "Wow! It's dark down there."

"Look!" said Lucy. She was pointing downstream. "Animals!"

"Raccoons!" said Uncle Pete. "Let's make tracks!" He moved faster.

"They don't know we're here, Uncle Pete," said Cousin Dinky. "The wind is blowing toward us so they can't smell us. Besides, they're busy feeding at the stream."

The tiny family hurried off the bridge and down the path away from the stream. When they got to the Longs' yard (where the Buttons lived) they heard a terrible racket.

"Everybody stop!" Mr. Little drew his needle sword.

"What is it?" Lucy whispered. She moved closer to her father.

"Cats!" Mr. Little said and he pointed to two shadowy humps just ahead. "Two of them. And from the way they sound, they are about to have a fight!"

"THOSE CATS are in our way," said Uncle Pete. "Can we go around them?"

"They're right in front of the secret door into the house," Cousin Dinky said.

"We might have to wait here until morning," Tom said. "Cats can sit and stare at each other for hours."

"I think we should wait here until they go away," Mrs. Little said.

"Well, I don't," said Uncle Pete. "Any good fighter knows it's better to do something than nothing."

"You think we should attack them?" said Mr. Little. He turned to Cousin

Dinky. "Can you imagine our starting a fight with two cats? I can't."

"No, no!" Uncle Pete said. "Just Dinky and I should attack. As the two most experienced fighters, we can keep them busy while the rest of you sneak past them into the house."

"Then what will happen to you?" Mr. Little said.

"Oh, we'll get away somehow," Uncle Pete said.

"Good heavens, Uncle Pete!" said Mr. Little. "This is no time to be a hero. The cats haven't seen us. Surely we're smarter than they are. We can find a way past them."

"I have an idea," said Tom.

"Good!" said Mr. Little. "Let's hear your idea, Tom."

"First we tie all the strings together to get one long string," Tom said. "Then we tie a balloon with its basket to one end of the string. We tie the other end to a bush. Someone gets in the basket. We let the balloon and basket go all the way up — as high as the string will let them go."

Tom took a deep breath. "While that's happening, the rest of the people get over near the secret door. Then the person in the balloon makes a hissing noise. The cats come over to see what it is and everybody runs for the secret door."

"And the man in the balloon," said Mr. Little. "What happens to him?"

"He'll be safe up in the air," Tom said. "The cats won't be able to get him. After they go away, he pulls himself down."

Everyone agreed that Tom's idea was the best and safest one for getting into the house.

Cousin Dinky said he would go up in the balloon. Tom begged to go with him.

Mrs. Little said, "He's too young. It may not be safe. I wish he wouldn't."

Mr. Little said, "Tom's not too young to think up a good idea to help his family. He can be trusted not to do anything foolish. I'm going to let him go with his cousin. It will be a good experience for him."

Granny Little whispered to Mrs. Little, "Dinky has had a thousand more dangerous adventures than going up in that balloon. He wouldn't take Tom with him if he didn't think he'd be perfectly safe."

"I'm really a coward," Mrs. Little whispered to Granny Little. "But I want Tom to be brave."

"He'll be all right," said Granny Little. She patted Mrs. Little's hand. "And you're not a coward. You're afraid sometimes — and who isn't?"

The Littles unloaded the balloon basket that carried the suitcases. They left the marbles in the basket. Then they loaded some of the suitcases into the other balloon basket and carried the rest.

"Let's move out and get nearer the house," Mr. Little said. "We'll stay out of the light of the moon and go through the garden so the cats don't see us. And no noise."

The tiny people started out.

"Please be careful, Tom," whispered Mrs. Little.

Cousin Dinky and Tom began to tie the strings together.

"Make square knots, Tom," Cousin Dinky said. "They won't slip."

Soon they had a piece of string eight feet long. They tied one end to the balloon basket and the other to a bush.

Tom and Cousin Dinky climbed aboard. They unloaded some marbles to lighten the weight. Soon the airship was rising.

"Let's make noises now!" Cousin Dinky said.

The two Littles hissed at the cats.

When the cats heard the noise they stopped fighting. They stretched their necks, sniffed, and turned toward the noise. They crouched down and sneaked across the yard to see what was going on.

As soon as the cats got near, Cousin Dinky and Tom stopped hissing. The cats walked back and forth, staring at the balloon.

Cousin Dinky and Tom waited quietly. By now the rest of the Littles were safely in the house. But the cats wouldn't go away.

"I hate to bop those poor cats," said Cousin Dinky. "I suppose we'll have to, since they won't leave." He picked up two marbles. "You aim for the one on the left, Tom. Fire when I say 'fire,' and try to hit him the first time. We want to give them a good scare."

Tom got two marbles and set himself to throw.

"Ready!" whispered Cousin Dinky. "Aim...fire! Bombs away."

"EEEEEOOOOOooowwwWWW!!!"

"YYYyyyyyyaaaaarrrrrRRR!!"

Swish! Swish! The cats ran off.

Silence.

"They're gone," Cousin Dinky said. "Tom, you and I are pretty good marble players."

Cousin Dinky began pulling on the string that held the balloon to the bush below. They moved slowly toward the ground.

Suddenly the string went limp. Cousin Dinky fell over backwards.

"What happened?" said Tom. He rushed to the edge of the basket. The ground seemed to be moving away from them.

"One of those knots didn't hold!" shouted Cousin Dinky. "The string broke!"

The balloon shot up. It was now above the trees and drifting with the wind.

Tom drew an arrow to his bow. He

aimed at the balloon. "We've got to let the gas out," he said.

"No, Tom, no!" said Cousin Dinky. He held his hand in front of the arrow. "It's a rubber balloon. It would rip apart. We'd be killed in the fall."

Cousin Dinky climbed up on the side of the basket. He reached for the cord tied to the opening of the balloon. The knot was a hard one. Cousin Dinky needed all his strength to untie it.

The balloon went higher, drifting with the wind. Houses were so far below they looked like toys.

Finally Cousin Dinky got the knot loose. "Wooossshhh!" Some of the gas escaped. The balloon began to drift down. Now Cousin Dinky had to hold the knot tight to keep gas from escaping too fast.

Slowly, slowly, the balloon settled down toward the ground. The tops of trees were even with the balloon.

Thump! The basket hit the ground. The cousins were tossed into a clump of grass.

"Well, Tom," Cousin Dinky said. "That was an unexpected adventure. Are you all right?"

Tom didn't answer. He was pointing to a pair of yellow eyes staring at them from under a bush.

MEANWHILE, at the Longs' house the Buttons were greeting the Littles.

Mrs. Button came to the door first. She had a pretty round face, and her eyes looked like shiny black buttons. "Oh, it's the Lit —"

"Well, well, WELL!!" Mr. Button's voice boomed behind her. "It's the Littles! What a wonderful visit! What wonderful people, the Littles!"

The tiny man's chubby red face was smiling and smiling. He hugged the women and gave the men strong hand-shakes.

Mrs. Button spotted Della Kett. "And this is Della Ke — "

Mr. Button didn't let his wife finish. "And here's Miss Della Kett," he said. "The beautiful bride-to-be."

"Della, the last time we saw you," Mr. Button went on, "you weren't any bigger than dear little Lucy Little." He patted Lucy on the head. She ducked out from under his hand.

"Now she's going to be married," said Mrs. Button.

"And now you're going to be married," said Mr. Button. "My, my, my, that's wonderful! *And,* you're going to be married to a fellow who is the salt of the earth — Dinky Little!"

Mrs. Button looked around. "Dinky isn't with you?"

"Dinky isn't with you!" Mr. Button said. He smiled his big smile. "We can't have a wedding without the bridegroom, can we? Where is the lucky lad?"

Mr. Little explained why Cousin Dinky and Tom were late.

"Oh, those awful cats!" Mrs. Button said. "Well, I'm sure Dinky and Tom can handle them." Then she smiled. "While we're waiting for the boys, you can start eating breakf — "

"Yes, YES!" Mr. Button broke in. "Mrs. Button has prepared a delicious breakfast of leftovers. Let's not keep Mrs. Button waiting, folks." He winked at Mr. Little. "My little woman has a terrible temper if you keep her waiting."

"I can see why she has a temper," Uncle Pete whispered to Granny Little. They walked toward the kitchen. "Old Button won't let his wife finish a sentence."

During breakfast everyone watched Baby Betsy. Mrs. Little sat her up in a high chair the Buttons kept for visiting

children. (They had no children of their own.) She was feeding her a slice of banana and a couple of corn flakes.

"She's adorable!" said Mrs. Button.

"Adorable!" echoed Mr. Button.

Uncle Pete groaned.

Baby Betsy grabbed the spoon out of her mother's hand and jerked it. Some of the banana and corn flakes landed on Uncle Pete's shirt.

"Isn't she a smart one?" said Uncle Pete. "She knows we're talking about her."

Lucy Little jumped out of her chair. She ran over and kissed Baby Betsy, then she ran back to her chair.

"Lucy!" said Granny Little. "Where did you get all that energy?"

"Where are those boys?" Mrs. Little said. "They should be here by now."

"Yes, they should," Mr. Little said.

The men decided to look for them.

Mr. Little, Mr. Button, and Uncle Pete left the Longs' house by the secret door. It was light now. The rising sun made long shadows in the yard. Mr. Little found a long piece of string at the bush where Cousin Dinky had tied the balloon.

Mr. Little held the end of the string in his hand. He looked at the sky. "The balloon is gone," he said. "Something went wrong."

"I should have stayed with them," Uncle Pete said.

"Look! All's well that ENDS WELL!!" Mr. Button shouted. He pointed to the edge of the Longs' yard.

"Well, I'll be," Uncle Pete said.

"Tom! Dinky!" Mr. Little called. "Thank heavens you're safe!"

The three tiny men ran across the yard.

Hildy, the Biggs' cat, walked slowly in their direction. She was carrying the two cousins on her back. They were laughing and cheering.

Cousin Dinky explained what had happened to them. ". . . and finally we landed right in front of two scary yellow eyes," he said, "that turned out to belong to our old friend, Hildy."

"Some luck!" Uncle Pete said.

"Some *cat!*" said Tom.

IT WAS almost time for the wedding. Everybody gathered in the Buttons' living room to make plans. They were wearing their finest clothes.

Della was beautiful in her white ruffled wedding dress. She carried one pink rosebud and her cheeks were pinker than the rose. Lucy, her flower girl, carried an acorn cap filled with three violets. They matched her blouse made of a French silk ribbon.

Mrs. Little, the matron of honor, wore a blue linen dress made from one of Mrs. Bigg's handkerchiefs. And Granny Little wore a yellow flowered dress made from the hat band of Mrs. Bigg's last year's Easter hat. Mrs. Button had on a tan lace dress. She had made it from a lace collar that Mrs. Long had thrown away.

Mr. Little explained how tiny people took part in the wedding ceremony. "Della and Dinky must stand as close to the big bride and groom as they can get. And, of course, the best man and the matron of honor must be with them," he said. "The rest of the tiny people may stand near these four if possible. If not possible, they may watch from any safe place in the room."

"Why do Della and Dinky have to stand so close to the big people?" Tom said.

"First — that is the custom, Tom," Mr. Little said. "And, second — so they'll be sure to hear the words when the minister says, 'Do you, Vera Long, take this man, Sam Tower, to be your husband.' At the *same time* Della must say, 'I Della Kett, take this man, Dinky Little, to be my husband. . . .' "

"Isn't it beautiful?" Mrs. Little said.

"It's important," Mr. Little went on, "for Della to speak loud enough for Dinky and the rest of us to hear her, but soft enough so the big people *don't* hear her. It's quite a trick."

"Do you have a place picked out for us to stand, Mr. Button?" Della said. "I'm dying to see it. Is it *very* near the big people?"

Mr. Button reached over and took Della's hand. "Your wedding will be held in the Longs' living room," he said. "And I have a nifty spot in mind for you. I think you'll love it."

Mr. Little looked at the watch over the fireplace. "We have about half an hour before the wedding begins. Shouldn't we get to our places now?"

"Follow me," Mr. Button said. "Let's see what's happening in the Longs' living room."

Tom whispered to Lucy. "I almost forgot — we have to move fast. We still don't have the ring."

Everybody left the apartment and hurried down the wall passageway to the Longs' living room. Tom and Lucy followed part of the way. When no one was looking, the two children turned off for Mrs. Long's bedroom.

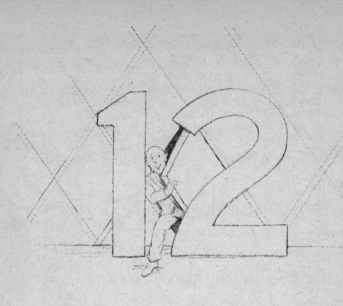

M R. BUTTON opened a trap door in the Longs' living room wall. He signaled for everyone to be quiet. Then he led them through the door.

They stood on the fireplace mantelpiece. The trap door was part of the wallpaper design. Mr. Button closed the door and no one could see it from the living room side.

Mr. Button whispered: "We are standing behind a clock on the mantelpiece. The clock looks like a house."

There was a small hole in the back of the clock. Mr. Button climbed through. "Follow me!" he whispered.

There was room to move around inside the clock without getting caught in the machinery. In the front of the clock-house were doors and windows. The Littles could see out into the Longs' living room where big people were moving around and talking.

There were wooden dolls standing in the doors and windows of the clock-house. They faced into the Longs' living room. The dolls looked like statues to the tiny people.

"Now here's my plan," Mr. Button said. "As you can see, we are very close to where the wedding is going to take place. If you look out, you can see the minister. He's the gentleman in the black suit."

The Littles looked and nodded.

"When the wedding march is played, the big bride and her father are going to walk into the living room and up to where the minister is standing right in front of this clock," Mr. Button said.

"How thrilling!" Della said.

"We will be able to see and hear everything that takes place," said Mr. Button. Then he chuckled. "Now here is my greatest idea." The tiny man took hold of a wooden statue that was standing at a window of the clock-house. He gave it a pull and it came loose from its holder on the floor.

"What are you up to, Button?" Uncle Pete said.

"Now, Dinky," said Mr. Button, "when I take this statue away from the window, I want you to take its place."

"Hold on there!" said Uncle Pete.

"Do you mean," Mr. Little said, "that you want Dinky to stand right in that window where all those big people can see him?"

"They may look at the clock, but they won't see Dinky," said Mr. Button. "People see what they expect to see. And no big person expects to see a six-inch human being standing in a clock."

"Are you sure?" Uncle Pete said.

"I've stood in these windows quite a few times myself, just to test it," Mr. Button said. "Even when a big person looks at the clock to see what time it is, he doesn't really pay attention to these statues. It's really quite amazing. Come on, Dinky, my boy! Try it!"

"I'm ready," said Cousin Dinky. He stood next to the window.

Mr. Button got a good hold on the statue. "All right," he said. "Get set — go!"

Mr. Button quickly moved the wooden statue away from the window. Cousin Dinky stepped into its place. He looked out at the living room. About fifteen people were sitting there. The minister stood in front of them with his back to Cousin Dinky. The people kept looking at the door and talking in low voices.

Mr. Button took another statue away. Della stepped into the place next to Cousin Dinky. Now, she too was watching what was going on in the Longs' living room.

"It's getting close to the time," Mr. Button said. "Let's get everyone into place." He pointed to a spot near Cousin Dinky. "The best man should stand here."

Uncle Pete moved into the place. "That's me," he said.

"And now, Mr. Little — you're giving the bride away," said Mr. Button. "You should stand here."

Mr. Little did as he was told.

"And the matron of honor goes about here," Mr. Button said.

Mrs. Little moved quickly into the place pointed out to her.

"Now — the ring bearer should stand next to the best man," said Mr. Button, "and the flower girl goes next to the matron of honor."

"The children aren't here," Mr. Little said. He looked around.

Uncle Pete ran to the back of the clock. He looked out. "I don't think they ever got here," he said.

"Oh dear," said Mrs. Little. "Tom has the ring."

"I'd better get them," Uncle Pete said, and he hurried out of the clock.

In the meantime Cousin Dinky and Della were still standing in the clock window. They tried to keep from moving.

The minister turned around and looked right at the clock. Then he looked at his wrist watch. Suddenly he turned and leaned on the mantelpiece. He was only a few inches away from Della and Cousin Dinky. They stood very still.

The minister began to examine the things on the mantelpiece as he waited for the wedding to begin. He looked at a photograph. He picked up a small bird made of glass.

Then, he looked the clock over carefully. Cousin Dinky and Della stood stiff as boards. The minister reached up and slowly ran his fingers over the top of the clock-house.

The people in the room kept on talking in low voices and looking at the door.

The minister reached right in front of the two tiny people. They stopped breathing! The man *touched* one of the wooden statues. Cousin Dinky saw the minister looking at him. He *knew* he was going to be next.

WHILE the wedding party was crowding into the clock-house, Tom and Lucy were in Mrs. Long's room looking for a ring.

The two tiny children crawled over a jumble of things on the woman's dresser. Lucy tripped backwards over a hair curler.

"Let's get going!" Tom said. "Get up — we have to hurry."

The children looked around the dresser top. "It has to be here somewhere," Tom said. "There! There it is." It was Mrs. Long's box for broken jewelry. The box was jammed with broken jewelry, beads, and buttons.

Tom dug around in the box for a few minutes. He pulled out a tiny round link for a chain. "This will fit Della's finger," he said.

"It's a little too thick, isn't it?" Lucy said.

"It's the best we're going to find," said Tom. "There's nothing in this box that is better. We don't have time to look anyplace else."

"Golly!" said Lucy. "We're always hurrying. Haste does make waste, I guess."

"Oh stop it, Lucy!" Tom said. "Don't be that way. Come on! Let's find some glue and stick the ruby on."

They found some glue in Mr. Long's desk. "It's some of that good white stuff that Mrs. Bigg uses," Tom said. "It really sticks."

Lucy stood on the tube of glue and squeezed a drop out. Tom took the ruby out of his pocket and glued it to the ring.

The children blew on the glue to make it dry faster.

"It looks pretty good," Lucy said. "I thought it was going to look beautiful."

"It *is* beautiful!" Tom said. "I'll make one just like it for you when you get married."

Just then they heard music.

"What's that?" said Tom.

"Listen!" Lucy said. Then she shouted. "That's the wedding march. We've got to get back." She started to run.

"Hold it, Lucy!" said Tom. "I just remembered. We don't even know where everybody is standing."

"Tom!" Lucy said. "We'll miss the wedding"

WHEN the wedding march began, the minister turned away from the clock on the mantelpiece.

Cousin Dinky looked over at Della. She looked at him and smiled.

The wedding march played on. The big groom, Sam Tower, stood with his best man in front of the minister. The people in the living room turned to watch the bride come walking into the living room with her father. They walked slowly, in time to the music. At last they came before the minister.

"*Dearly beloved, we are gathered together...*" the minister said.

"Where are those children and Uncle Pete?" Mr. Little whispered.

"We'll just have to get along without them," Mr. Button said.

"But Tom is supposed to have the ring!" Mr. Little said.

"*Into this holy estate,*" the minister was saying, "*these two persons present now come to be joined.*"

"Tom had a ruby, I know that," Mrs. Little said. "Did he ever find a ring to put it on?"

"I never thought about asking him," Mr. Little said. "He usually does what he says he'll do."

"*...let him now speak or else hereafter forever hold his peace,*" said the minister.

"Oh dear, whatever are we going to do if there's no ring?" said Mrs. Little.

"*Wilt thou have this woman to thy wedded wife?*" the minister went on.

"*I will!*" said Sam Tower in the living room.

"*I will!*" said Cousin Dinky in the clock.

"I'd better go see if I can find those children," Mr. Button said.

"Somebody had better do something," said Mr. Little.

"*Wilt thou have this man to thy wedded husband?*" the minister said.

"*I will!*" Vera Long said.

"*I will!*" whispered Della.

The minister came to the part in the ceremony where he asked: "*Who giveth this woman to be married to this man?*" Mr. Long placed Vera Long's hand in the minister's hand. The minister had Sam Tower take Vera's hand.

At the same time, Mr. Little took Della's hand and placed it in Cousin Dinky's hand. Cousin Dinky and Della smiled at each other.

"*I, Dinky, take thee, Della, to my wedded wife,*" Cousin Dinky said, echoing what was being said in the living room.

Then it was Della's turn. *"I, Della,"* she said, *"take thee, Dinky, to my wedded husband."*

Just then, Tom and Lucy came running into the clock. Mr. Button was behind them. Tom held out the ruby ring. Mr. Little took it and handed it to Cousin Dinky, who slipped it onto Della's finger.

"With this ring, I do thee wed," said Cousin Dinky.

Della was almost laughing. Her pink cheeks got even pinker. *Tick-tock* went the clock. Suddenly bells struck the half hour. The tiny people held their ears.

The minister finished the ceremony. *"Those whom God hath joined together let no man put asunder."*

Sam Tower kissed Vera Tower.

Cousin Dinky Little kissed Della Little.

Uncle Pete came back at last. "Oh, here's everyone!" he said.

"You missed the wedding," said Granny Little.

"Oh, my golly," Uncle Pete said. "I did!" Then he walked over to Della. "I was the last to get here. May I be the first to kiss the bride?"

And he was.

There are more books about the Littles
you may want to read:

The Littles
The Littles Take a Trip
The Littles to the Rescue
The Littles Give a Party
   (Former title: *The Littles' Surprise Party*)
Tom Little's Great Halloween Scare
The Littles and the Trash Tinies
The Littles and the Big Storm
The Littles Go Exploring
The Littles and Their Friends

All Littles books are published in paperback
by Scholastic Book Services.